The Knight and the Squire

The Knight

A retelling of the adventures of
Don Quixote and Sancho Panza
based on Cervantes'
Don Quixote de la Mancha

and the Squire

by *Argentina Palacios*

illustrated by **Ray Cruz**

Doubleday & Company, Inc., Garden City, New York

*To the memory of the one
who introduced me to
the Knight and the Squire,
my maternal grandfather,
Don Santos George Ruiz.*

Library of Congress Cataloging in Publication Data

Palacios, Argentina.
The knight and the squire.

SUMMARY: An abridged version of the adventures of a
Spanish country gentleman, considered mad, and his
companion who set out as knights of old to right wrongs
and punish evil.
[1. Knights and knighthood—Fiction.   2. Spain—
Fiction]   I. Cruz, Ray.   II. Cervantes Saavedra,
Miguel de, 1547–1616. Don Quixote.   III. Title.
PZ7.P1753Kn   [Fic]
ISBN: 0-385-12433-3 Trade
ISBN: 0-385-12434-1 Prebound
Library of Congress Catalog Card Number 78–20091

Contents

CHAPTER 1

A Knight in Armor

Once, there was a man who went crazy from too much reading. He only read books about knighthood; that was the problem. Those books told about the adventures of knights in armor, their fantastic encounters with dragons, monsters, giants, wizards, and even other knights. There was also talk of love, because each knight had a lady of his dreams.

Soon the man came to believe that all those fantastic tales were true. One day, he decided to become a knight too, for he wanted to right all that was wrong in the world, and punish evil. Alone in his room, he practiced jousting. Wham wham wham! Like the heroes in his books, he always won.

All this happened in a little village in a province called La Mancha, in the heart of Spain. The man had lived in the same place all his life, as his parents and grandparents had before him. He was about fifty, tall and thin, and he had a small beard. No one would ever expect anything bad from him or think anything wrong about him, for he was an honorable man, a perfect gentleman. Two other people lived in his home: his pretty, cheerful, innocent niece of about twenty;

and his plump housekeeper, about forty, a good, friendly soul with strong opinions about everything. A boy served as handyman around the house.

It is not clear what the gentleman's real name was. Some think it was Alonso Quixano, but the last name could have been Quixada, Quesada, or Quexana. He came from a respectable family—that's why he was called *Don* Alonso. There was a little land in the estate, very little else. When he became ill, he began selling many acres of good farm land to buy more of his favorite books.

One day, the actual preparations to become a knight began. Somewhere in the house there was an old suit of armor that had belonged to his great-grandfather. He cleaned, polished, and fixed it up as best he could. The helmet was in such bad shape, it had to be tied together. A horse he already had—old and bony, not much of a horse, but a mount nonetheless. He spent four whole days thinking of a good name for his horse. It would be Rocinante. And what a good name it was! *Rocín* is a Spanish word that means "nag" or "work horse"; and *antes* means "before." To most people, the name means "This was once a horse," but to Don Alonso, it meant a steed *above* and *beyond* all other horses in the world!

His own name, Don Alonso, didn't seem good enough for a knight. He changed it to Don Quixote, and added de la Mancha so everyone would know where he came from. Don Quixote de la Mancha. What a fine-sounding name for a knight!

But he still needed a lady, a lady to dream about, a

lady to receive homage from his defeated enemies. No one knew he was in love, but he was . . . so secretly, it seems, that even the lady herself didn't know he liked her! She was a farm girl from nearby El Toboso, and she was plain, rough, ordinary. Her name was Aldonza Lorenzo. He had seen her only once in his life. Without her knowledge, Don Quixote pronounced her his "lady" and called her Dulcinea del Toboso. Her name, like the others, was right: it comes from the Spanish word *dulce,* which means "sweet."

Don Quixote was very pleased with his preparations.

CHAPTER 2

Don Quixote Leaves Home

Before sunup the next morning, Don Quixote left, destination unknown. At home, they didn't know he was leaving. He rode happily through the dry, flat land for a while, until he suddenly remembered he had not been properly knighted. He could not engage in combat if he was not a dubbed knight. He thought hard, and at last found the solution: he would continue on his way and ask the first person he met to do him the honor and dub him a knight!

It was July, a scorching month in Spain. Neither heat nor thirst stopped Don Quixote; there was only adventure in his mind. By sundown, he and Rocinante were tired and hungry. And then a light shone in the distance. "How lucky I am!" he said to himself. "A castle . . . I can see the moat from here . . . and on the other side, three or four imposing turrets." Toward that "castle" they went.

It wasn't a castle, of course, just a simple country inn. Instead of a page to announce his arrival, there were two ordinary women at the door—two women who had never seen a knight or heard about knighthood before. The strange sight of Rocinante and Don Quixote frightened them at first.

"Look at that!" one said. "What is it?"

"Let's run inside," said the other. "It looks danger-ous!"

"Your Highnesses, beautiful princesses, there is nothing to be afraid of," Don Quixote assured them. "I am a knight in armor who will do you no harm. I am here to see the exalted lord of this magnificent castle."

That old-fashioned language surprised the women. Seconds later, though, they thought this must be a joke, a very funny joke, because this was no castle and they were no princesses. They laughed and laughed at his looks and at his speech, until the innkeeper came out to see what was going on. Don Quixote was al-lowed to stay.

As for dinner, the only thing left was some ill-cooked codfish and stale bread. For the starving knight, this was a banquet. He tried to drink some wine. Catastrophe! There was wine spilled all over. He had kept his helmet on, because he could not undo the many knots he had tied to keep it on. The people at the inn improvised a drinking straw out of a reed; only then could he drink. It was a sight very much out of the ordinary!

After dinner, Don Quixote told the innkeeper his "secret," and asked him to dub him a knight. The inn-keeper didn't want to, at first. Then he decided to have a little fun, and agreed. There was a small prob-lem, Don Quixote was told; "the castle's chapel" was "being rebuilt." So the ceremony would have to take place in the courtyard.

First there was the watching of the armor. In this

part of the ceremony, the knight had to honor his
armor by standing guard over it. Don Quixote paced
back and forth in the moonlight, with most of the
guests as an audience.

Also staying at the inn that night were a group of
mule drivers. It so happened that about that hour was
the normal time to give water to their mules. But Don
Quixote had placed his armor over the water tank!

One of the mule drivers started to move the armor, and Don Quixote cried out: "You evil creature! What are you doing?"

The mule driver went on with his business. He didn't even look at the knight.

"Keep your hands off my armor!" Don Quixote said as he attacked in a wild rage.

Then a second mule driver came to the water tank. But before he could even touch the armor, Don Quixote attacked him, this time in complete silence.

The rest of the mule drivers couldn't just stand by and watch. It was their turn. That could have been the end of Don Quixote, such a beating they gave him. But the innkeeper managed to calm everybody down, and he decided to conclude the ceremony immediately, before something worse happened. Pretending that a book he used to keep his accounts was a prayer book, the innkeeper sang a couple of psalms and finished the ceremony.

The sword was handed to Don Quixote and his spurs were buckled. He also received a ceremonial blow with the side of the sword on neck and back. A true knight at last! He mounted Rocinante, gave his most heartfelt thanks, and left the inn. It was just before sunup.

CHAPTER 3

The Price of Meddling

Don Quixote was going back home, mainly because of a conversation he and the innkeeper had had before the dubbing ceremony.

"Tell me, Sir Knight, how much money do you have with you?" the innkeeper asked.

"I beg your pardon, my lord. I carry none," Don Quixote answered. "It is not the custom of knights in armor to carry money with them. No book about knighthood I ever read mentions it."

"Oh, Sir Knight, it is too obvious a matter to be mentioned. All knights carry money, believe me, it's a necessity," the innkeeper said with great feeling.

Though he would not say it, the innkeeper was worried about not being paid. But he liked to joke, too, so he continued: "When I was young, I myself was interested in becoming a knight. I also know that knights carry a change of clothes and a small first-aid kit." He paused for a second, then added: "You, like all knights in armor, should have a squire to be your helper and companion."

Don Quixote, with his fantasy-filled mind, didn't find a hidden meaning in the conversation or see that the innkeeper was making fun of him. He planned to follow the innkeeper's advice to the letter.

Suddenly Don Quixote heard voices coming from a nearby bush; they sounded like a person's moans. And moans they were. A boy of about fifteen was tied to a tree, naked from the waist up. He was being whipped by a man. Don Quixote stopped to see what was wrong, and he learned that the man was a rich farmer and the boy tended one of his flocks of sheep. The farmer was punishing the boy for not doing his job right, or so he said. Don Quixote learned that the man owed the boy some back pay, so he figured out how much it was and, with lance menacing, ordered the farmer to pay what he owed.

"Fine, Sir Knight; I am ready to pay him, but I have no money with me," the farmer said. "Andrew should come home with me to get his money." And to Andrew: "Please do come with me, brother."

"So, you see, young man, everything will be fine," Don Quixote told Andrew.

"Oh, no, Sir Knight," Andrew replied, "my master will skin me alive first."

"Young man," Don Quixote said, "your master has given his word and I trust that he will keep it. If he doesn't, I'll come back and make him regret it, and he'll have to pay double!"

Don Quixote then left, thinking that the farmer (and everyone else) was as honorable as himself. But as soon as the knight was out of their sight, the beating became twice as hard. "Ha ha ha, go get your sav-

ior, Andrew," the farmer taunted. And Andrew wished the well-meaning gentleman had not meddled.

Meanwhile, Don Quixote had met other people farther up the road, some merchants and their servants. The knight planted himself in the middle of the road, challenging every one of those "knights" to fight, one by one or in a group.

"We are peaceful people, sir; we are merchants, we are not knights," they said.

"You are cowards who don't want to face a lone knight, that's what you are!" he taunted.

One of the servants threw a stone at Don Quixote. Many more stones followed . . . and a very bruised Don Quixote fell flat on the ground. He couldn't move an inch. But he didn't feel sorry for himself, not for one minute. He knew that all knights in armor had a little bad luck now and then. To pass the time, he began singing old ballads and romances he remembered.

As luck would have it, a neighbor of his was traveling the same road, on business. After removing some of the armor and grime, the man recognized Don Alonso and took him back to town.

At home there was quite a stir. Before Don Alonso had become Don Quixote, he had had two good friends: the village priest and the village barber. That evening, the priest and the barber came to the house: the niece and the housekeeper needed to be comforted, and they also needed to figure out how to find the missing person.

"Oh, why didn't I tell you about those cursed books

of knighthood?" asked the housekeeper over and over. And the niece: "I peeked through the keyhole a couple of times. Uncle was stabbing the walls—killing giants is what he said. I know those books drove him crazy, I know it, I'm sure. We should do something about those hateful books!"

But before they could do anything, the neighbor entered with the missing knight in tow.

Don Quixote didn't know who they were or where he was. He said a giant had beaten him up. Everyone's fears were confirmed now: he had lost his senses, no doubt about it. They put him to bed, fed him, and took care of his bruises. He kept singing his ballads until he fell asleep.

The next morning, while their friend was still asleep, the priest and the barber returned. The two of them helped the women burn the books. They tossed the valuable books into the courtyard and made a huge bonfire with them. Then they agreed to tell him —if he asked—that a wizard came in a smoke cloud and took all the books. He did ask, and that's what he was told.

After the books were burned, they thought everything would go back to normal. How misguided they were!

CHAPTER 4

Don Quixote and Sancho Panza Have Some Strange Adventures

The next two weeks were rather quiet at home. The priest and the barber spent long hours chatting with their friend, just as they had in the good old days. Everyone thought the insanity was gone now. What no one knew was that sometime during those days Don Quixote had talked to a neighbor, usually a sensible man, and had filled his head with crazy ideas.

His name was Sancho Panza. He was short and stout, a simple man who didn't know how to read and write. Sancho was a poor farmer with a wife, a son, and a daughter. He loved his family and worked hard. But now his neighbor—who knew a lot—was promising great things if Sancho went traveling with him. "In the old days," Don Quixote had said, "knights won islands and kingdoms. They gave them to their squires to govern. I plan to do the same with you, Sancho, if you become my squire."

Sancho thought this over and over. An island to

govern! He said to himself: "I'd be rich! I'll never have anything if I stay home and work non-stop for the rest of my life! I can send money to my family from the island."

So it was that, late one night, without saying good-by to wife or children, niece or housekeeper, the two adventurers left unnoticed. Don Quixote, again on his Rocinante; Sancho, on the only mount he had, a grayish donkey he called Rucio because of its color. On his master's advice, the squire had taken big saddlebags full of food and other provisions. They rode all night and stopped only at dawn, when they were sure they couldn't be found.

Sancho's mind was fixed on one thing: that island. How long would it be in coming? he wanted to know. It could be any time, maybe within six days, his master said.

On the road again after a while, they caught a glimpse of thirty or forty windmills, a common sight in those parts. Don Quixote thought this was wonderful.

"Look yonder, Sancho; there are thirty or more monstrous giants. I shall engage them in fierce combat. And when I win, Sancho, we'll be on our way to riches with the spoils."

"What giants, Your Grace?" asked Sancho.

"Those yonder, those of the long arms," his master replied.

"But, Your Grace, they're not giants. They're windmills!" Sancho warned. "There are no arms, just the sails going with the wind."

"It is crystal clear, Sancho, that you don't know

what you're saying," Don Quixote affirmed. "If you are afraid, stand to the side. Let me fight them alone."

"Master, master . . . they are windmills! They are not giants, master. THEY ARE WINDMILLS . . . WINDMILLS!"

The knight didn't hear his squire's urgent cries. He rushed toward the windmills, challenging and insulting the big white things all the while. Just then, the wind blew and the sails began to go around. "You don't frighten me!" he told them. At Rocinante's fastest gallop, he charged and lanced a sail. The wind made the sail go furiously: horse and knight were thrown far afield.

Sancho rushed to help. "God in heaven! Didn't I tell you, master, they were windmills?"

"Hush, Sancho, my friend. Matters of war, more than others, are subject to change," Don Quixote told him. "It was my old enemy the wizard Frestón who turned the giants into windmills. He did not want me to win."

"May it be the Almighty's will," said a resigned Sancho as he helped his master rise and mount poor, bruised Rocinante.

* * *

That night, the knight and his squire camped in a nearby forest. The next day, they headed for the mountain pass of Lápice. There would be a lot of adventure there, for sure. A couple of friars riding mules (to Don Quixote, "horses as big as dromedaries") were approaching. Behind them, but not with them, came a stagecoach escorted by four or five horsemen. A lady, traveling with her maids, was on her way to Seville to meet her husband.

"Aha, I have them now," Don Quixote said to himself. And then to the friars: "You wicked wizards, you won't be able to kidnap that lovely princess and her lovely ladies in waiting!"

"Sir, we are two innocent friars; we haven't kidnaped anyone," one of them protested.

"That's a disguise," Don Quixote said. "But you can't hide from me."

The horsemen accompanying the women had had enough. There was fighting, a tremendous free-for-all. Poor Sancho got a mean beating. The worst part, though, was when one of the horsemen, a huge fellow, decided to go after Don Quixote. It was obvious he intended to kill the strange old man. But as he was about to charge, he fell off his horse. It was the knight's day, and he was ready to take revenge.

"Sir Knight, we beg you, don't kill him!" the lady in the stagecoach cried.

Don Quixote stopped, went to the carriage, and ceremoniously said to her:

"I am sparing the man's life, most gracious princess, only because Your Highness has asked."

He commanded the fallen man: "You must now go to El Toboso to tell the most beautiful woman in the world, my lady Dulcinea, that I, the brave Don Quixote de la Mancha, defeated you to honor her."

This was one more thing to bewilder everyone, especially the horseman. Knights knew about paying homage to a lady, but he did not. And besides, who was this "lady" Dulcinea? Where was she? Neither the horseman nor anyone else dared to ask.

CHAPTER 5

More Strange Adventures

Knight and squire were on the road again when it started raining. A man with a shiny object on his head was coming toward them.

"Sancho, my friend, I am in luck," said Don Quixote. "I see the golden helmet of Mambrino on that man's head. That helmet is very valuable, you know."

"What golden helmet, my master?" Sancho asked. "I see something shiny, but that's no helmet."

"Sancho, you know nothing of knighthood! It may not *look* like a helmet to you, but to me . . . oh, I recognize it . . . the enchanted helmet I shall claim for myself."

Don Quixote charged. The man, scared to death, fell off his donkey and ran for his life.

The knight managed to untie his own headpiece, and put on the "helmet." It was too big, and a piece of it was missing. This was no golden helmet, of course, but a brass barber's basin. The barber was on his way to a house call; he'd worn the basin to protect his head from the rain.

"Oh, some ignoramus has melted a piece of this precious helmet for the gold," Don Quixote said. Sancho wanted to laugh but was afraid to; he'd seen his master get angry, and that could mean trouble. He wanted to laugh because this, like all barber's basins, had been made with a half-moon carved out to fit comfortably against the curve of a man's neck.

Knight and squire rode peacefully for a while, until they saw a gang of twelve chained men coming in their direction, with two guards in front and two in back. Sancho said they were prisoners on their way to do hard labor on the king's galley ships. "They'll have to row those ships," he said. "I've heard that prisoners dread the big oars."

"Do you mean they're going against their will?" asked Don Quixote. "I will never let that happen!"

The knight stopped the group and asked a number of questions. One was a robber, another a horse thief; a third was an embezzler. The worst criminal of all, with many counts against him, was a man named Ginés de Pasamonte, who, on top of it all, was cocky and arrogant.

"You men are being punished for your bad behavior," Don Quixote told the convicts, "but since I know you don't want to go where you're being taken, I'll ask this guard to set you free."

"That's just what we need now!" exclaimed the guard. "Sir, we don't have the authority to set them free. Go with God, and stop looking for trouble."

"You're the one looking for trouble," Don Quixote said as he attacked the guard. The other guards came to defend their colleague . . . and the criminals broke loose.

"Hear, all you newly free men, you must pay me for the favor I've done you," said Don Quixote to the scattering men. "Go to El Toboso and show the chains to my lady Dulcinea. Tell her, step by step, how I, her ardent suitor, the brave Don Quixote de la Mancha, set you free. After that, you may go wherever you want."

"We can't all go together," said Ginés de Pasamonte. "We'd be caught again. And as for taking up those chains once more, you must be joking! That's out of the question!"

"Well, then, Ginés, you shall do it alone, in everybody's name," Don Quixote said.

"Oh, yes? I shall do this, and this, and this," he said as he threw stones at Don Quixote. He motioned for the other convicts to do the same. A shower of stones for Don Quixote and Sancho was the reward. Then the criminals all fled, each in a different direction.

Donkey, horse, squire, and knight were thrashed without mercy. Don Quixote was extremely sad. Such ingratitude! he thought. And from the very people he had helped the most. He recovered quickly, however, and his thoughts soon turned again to other ways he could help people in need.

CHAPTER 6

Back to La Mancha Again

One day, Don Quixote decided to go into the mountains of Sierra Morena for a while. He wanted to be alone to think of his life and love, to gather his thoughts. Sancho was sent to deliver a letter to Dulcinea.

It was August now, almost a month since they had left home. The priest and the barber had taken to the road to find them. And Sancho ran into them!

"Sancho, where's your master? You haven't killed him, have you?" the priest asked.

"Oh, no, Your Grace; my master is safe and sound deep in that mountain," Sancho said. "He's just a little strange sometimes, talking to Lady Dulcinea; you'd think she's right there next to him."

"Well, it is important for the two of you to go back home," said the priest.

"His estate needs attention; you yourself would be better off helping your wife take care of the fields," the barber chimed in.

"With all due respect, you don't understand," Sancho said. "Master and I go around righting things that are wrong in the world and fighting evil."

"Sancho, Sancho, you're beginning to sound like your master. Of course we understand; that's why we want both of you to go back home. There are wrongs to right at home, too," the priest said.

"Sancho, go back to the mountain," the barber commanded. "Tell your master anything you like, but bring him down from the mountain. We'll wait at the foot. Don't tell him you saw us. We'll be in disguise when you come out."

Sancho went to bring his master. The friends followed a short distance behind. They soon met a runaway young woman, who, after a brief explanation, agreed to help in bringing the old gentleman home. Her assignment: to play a princess, Micomicona, who had come all the way from Africa, seeking Don Quixote's help. The story went like this: Her father had been dethroned by a mean giant. She had heard about Don Quixote's bravery. She knew he was the only one who could help her. When she became queen, she'd give him a huge reward. On hearing the tale, Don Quixote was delighted. Sancho was astonished. (An island to govern, at last! he thought.)

The group came to an inn. Don Quixote and Sancho went to bed early. In a little while, Sancho ran to the others, who were still up chatting and telling stories.

"Come, everybody! My master just killed the giant, the enemy of Princess Micomicona!" he said.

They ran to the room. Don Quixote was in a rage, stabbing a "giant," shouting, insulting him. "From this day on, Your Highness, you are free. The giant who

dethroned your father the King is dead!" he said to the "princess."

The innkeeper was beside himself. He kept the wine for the inn in wineskins, enormous containers made out of animal skins. He stored them in that room. Don Quixote had cut open the wineskins, thinking they were giants. What a loss! Sancho was just as unhappy: his hopes for an island were gone!

The priest and the barber had a wooden cage built in a hurry. It was large enough to hold a person. A few hours later, while the exhausted Don Quixote was still asleep, they grabbed him and put him in the cage. They were disguised, and told Don Quixote he was under a spell. Don Quixote took it all in stride, but Sancho was more than a little suspicious.

They got home in the middle of the day. It was as if the circus had arrived in town! The children ran to tell the housekeeper. Word got to Teresa Panza, Sancho's wife.

"How's the donkey, husband?" was the first thing she asked.

"In better shape than his owner," Sancho replied.

"Well, husband, what did you bring me? What did you bring the children? Clothing? Shoes?" she asked.

"None of that, woman, but something more valuable," he answered. "The next time my master and I go away, I'll come back governor of an island. You'll be rich."

"I hope so. . . . But, what did you say, what island?" Teresa wanted to know.

"Be in no hurry, wife," Sancho told her. "You'll know at the right time. You'll be called 'Excellency'!"

In the meantime, the niece and the housekeeper had put Don Quixote to bed. He didn't know where he was; he didn't know who they were.

The priest advised the women to keep an eye on him: he might want to take off again. The women cursed those confounded novels of knighthood for the millionth time.

CHAPTER 7

Don Quixote Learns He Is Already Famous

One month had gone by since Don Quixote had come back home, and his friends still had not seen him. The priest and the barber were everyday callers, but they were afraid he might remember past events if he saw either one of them. Sancho, of course, wasn't allowed in the house. And how desperately he wanted to see his master! One day, he almost made it inside before the niece and the housekeeper caught him trying to sneak in.

"What are you doing in this house, you beast?" yelled the housekeeper. "Haven't you done enough damage yet? You're responsible for taking Master away and doing all those crazy things."

"Evil, forked-tongue housekeeper, the one who's been talked into going is me," he said. "Your master told me a lot of things that weren't true. He even promised to give me an island to govern, and I'm still waiting for it."

"No matter; go away! Go take care of your household and your field," the niece commanded.

Such loud conversation was not missed by Don Quixote. He called Sancho in. "I am sorry, Sancho, that you feel I have misled you," his master told him. "We left together, we traveled together, we suffered together. I did not deceive you intentionally. You must agree that fortune was not with us. Now tell me, what have you heard about me? Tell me everything, without adding or subtracting a word."

"Fine, Your Grace," Sancho said, "but promise me you won't get angry at me."

"I won't; it's a promise," said the gentleman.

Then Sancho told him. "Well, there are many opinions about you in this town. Some say, 'He's crazy but funny'; others, 'He's brave but unfortunate'; others, 'He's polite but meddlesome.' And there's more! You remember the son of Bartholomew Carrasco, Samson, don't you? He came back from Salamanca yesterday—he just graduated from the university. I went to say hello to him, and he told me there's already a book about you . . . and I'm mentioned in it, and Lady Dulcinea is mentioned, and a whole lot of what's happened to us!"

Don Quixote wanted to meet Samson. Sancho went to the Carrasco home.

Samson was about twenty-four years old. He was a small man and not particularly good-looking. His mind was very quick, though, and he had a tremendous sense of humor. When he saw Don Quixote, he knelt on one knee, took Don Quixote's hand, and kissed it while he said, "It is with the most humble heart that I salute you, noble knight, one of the most famous in

the world. I cannot become tired of reading the story
of your adventures. I would be happy to be your ser-
vant."

Don Quixote asked him to rise and take a seat next
to him. They discussed at length the book Samson
liked to read. Don Quixote was very pleased with
what he heard. Sancho was beside himself with joy.

The young university graduate and the old gentleman became fast friends. Samson became a member of
the small circle and now joined the priest and the barber on their regular visits to Don Quixote.

CHAPTER 8

On the Road Again

The niece and the housekeeper thought Sancho was spending too much time in Don Quixote's room, behind closed doors. They suspected the two were planning to leave again, but they had no way to prove it or to stop them. Night came. Knight and squire left again, one for the third time, the other for the second. Destination: El Toboso. Purpose: to seek Dulcinea's blessings.

They arrived in El Toboso late the following evening. All was quiet; there was no one to tell them where Dulcinea lived. And even if there had been people around to ask, how would anyone know about "Dulcinea," a lady produced by Don Quixote's imagination? There was a real farm girl somewhere, but her name wasn't Dulcinea, and the gentleman had seen her only once before.

They rode around the deserted streets until near dawn, when they saw a farm hand going to work. Don Quixote stopped him. "Say, good man, could you tell us where is the palace of the beautiful princess Doña Dulcinea del Toboso?"

"Sir, I don't know," the man replied. "I'm from out

of town; I'm only working here for a while. The priest and the sexton live in that house across the street. They might know. . . . Hmm . . . but I don't think there's a princess living in this village."

Daylight had come. Don Quixote stayed hidden in a nearby bush while Sancho went to look for the lady he had never seen. Don Quixote asked him to come back quickly.

"What will I do?" Sancho thought. "How can I get out of this one?"

Then he saw three farm girls riding toward him. He ran back to Don Quixote.

"Master, master, Mistress Dulcinea and two other ladies are coming to see you!" he exclaimed.

"You are making fun of me, Sancho," his master said.

"Master, why would I do that? Come out, see for yourself. . . . They're beautiful!" Sancho insisted.

Don Quixote got out of the bush. He saw those less than glamorous women.

"Are they far, Sancho?" he asked.

"What do you mean, 'far'? Can't you see them, almost next to you?" Sancho replied.

Sancho grabbed the reins of one of the donkeys. Getting on his knees, he said, "Queen and princess and duchess of beauty! My name is Sancho Panza. I am the squire of that passionate knight you see next to me, the brave Don Quixote de la Mancha, who is in love with you!"

Don Quixote had gotten on his knees next to the girls.

"Dulcinea" was terribly annoyed. What nonsense! They were wasting time, and there was all that work to be done at the field.

"Shut up and move!" she snapped. "We're in a hurry! Move!"

"Won't you soften a little, lovely princess and queen of El Toboso?" Sancho pleaded.

"What do these town folks think we are?" one of the other girls said angrily. "You'd better move or our donkeys will walk all over you!"

Don Quixote moved and asked Sancho to move. Ah, those enchanters! They had done it again. They had just turned lovely Dulcinea into a gross, ordinary, ugly farm girl.

Sancho was relieved. He had gotten away with that one!

CHAPTER 9

The Knight of the Wood

Don Quixote and Sancho were sleeping in the woods when a noise awakened them. Two men had come on horseback. One of them got off and invited the other to stay. There was good grass for the horses, and peace and quiet for thought, he said.

Don Quixote looked carefully. One of them was wearing armor!

"Sancho, my brother, adventure is before us!" he said.

The other knight heard voices and asked who was there. Don Quixote answered, and they got together. The two squires took off in another direction.

"The life of a squire is indeed hard, isn't it?" the new squire said.

"It wouldn't be so bad if we ate regularly," Sancho replied.

The other one took food out of his saddlebag and they shared it. Then they watched the stars for a while and fell asleep.

Their masters were neither eating nor sleeping. The other knight, who called himself The Knight of the Wood, said to Don Quixote: "The proudest moment of my life came when I defeated that famous knight Don

Quixote de la Mancha. I made him confess that my lady Casildea is more beautiful than his Dulcinea."

"I don't doubt that you have defeated the bravest knights in all Spain, but not Don Quixote de la Mancha," the selfsame said. "Maybe someone who *looked* like him, but not him."

"Oh, no? I can prove it to you: he's tall, thin, has a pointy nose, a big fallen mustache, and grayish hair," the other knight boasted. "His squire is a farmer by the name of Sancho Panza. His horse is named Rocinante, and the lady of his dreams is Dulcinea del Toboso."

"It is absolutely false that you have defeated Don Quixote de la Mancha! I am Don Quixote de la Mancha, and you have never defeated me. I'll prove it to you with the strength of my arms!"

"So will I, as soon as day breaks," his opponent said confidently.

Sancho was speechless when he heard the news. A duel! He feared for his master. The other squire suggested they, too, fight while their masters fought. That was the custom in his homeland, he said. Sancho replied he was not going to fight—he had been a peaceful man all his life and intended to remain one.

In broad daylight, Sancho saw an enormous nose on the other squire. "This time it must really be some kind of magic!" he thought. Don Quixote, on the other hand, could not see his opponent's face, but he did see his armor. It was completely covered with tiny mirrors. He noticed, too, that the knight was a small man carrying an enormous lance.

"The condition of our fight is that the winner will decide the fate of the loser," The Knight of the Wood said.

"Agreed," Don Quixote answered.

Sancho climbed a tree to see the battle better—or, as Don Quixote accused him later, "to have a better view without any danger."

They fought. Don Quixote easily defeated the other knight. The fallen man looked dead. His squire—without the horrible nose—came running. So did Sancho, who wanted his master to kill the challenging knight. But then they saw the very figure of Samson Carrasco, the university graduate. And without the false nose, they discovered Tomé Cecial, Sancho's neighbor!

The Knight of the Wood came to. Don Quixote put the sword to his chest. He made his opponent confess that Dulcinea was far superior and more beautiful than his Casildea. That they looked like Samson Carrasco and Tomé Cecial puzzled him a bit for a moment, but he concluded that they were not really those they seemed to be. "Oh, they're just look-alikes sent by the enchanters. My enemies relish confusing me," he said.

But, of course, there was no enchantment involved. Samson had planned the scheme, thinking that he could easily defeat his friend and make him go back home. Unfortunately for Samson, he had been very wrong.

CHAPTER 10

The Adventure of the Lions

Victory had a sweet taste. That taste was still with Don Quixote when they met a gentleman wearing a green overcoat. They decided to travel together, since they were going in the same direction.

The knight and the gentleman began a lively conversation. They talked about the man's family, what everyone did, and how his son who was a student had decided to become a poet. It didn't take long for the man in the green coat to think that his new friend was crazy.

Sancho wasn't interested in their talk, however. He saw some shepherds milking their sheep at the side of the road and took a small detour to talk to them. The shepherds also had cottage cheese for sale and Sancho bought some. About the same time, Don Quixote spotted a small caravan flying royal banners. He called his squire, because Sancho had the helmet. Sancho didn't have time to eat the cottage cheese. Since he didn't know what to do with it, he stuffed it in his master's helmet.

Don Quixote put the helmet on. The whey from the

cottage cheese started to drip! Somewhat frightened, he asked Sancho for a cloth to clean himself with. Then he took the helmet off and smelled.

"You traitor and bad friend, this is one of your dirty tricks," he yelled at Sancho. "You put cottage cheese in my helmet. And I thought there was something seriously wrong with me!"

Sancho said sheepishly: "Master, if it's cottage cheese, give it to me, and I'll eat it. But believe me, master, I don't know how that got in there. I think that some wizard must be after me, too, for being your squire."

And as usual, Don Quixote blamed his "enemies." "Everything is possible, Sancho," he said.

Their traveling companion could not believe what he had just seen and heard . . . until he saw what came next.

The oxcart with royal banners was at their side now. With it came a cart driver and another man. Don Quixote planted himself in the middle of the road, blocking their way.

"Where to, brothers? What are you carrying in that oxcart? What do those banners mean?" he asked the men.

"The cart is mine," the driver answered. "I'm transporting two brave lions to the Court. They are a gift to the King. The banners mean that the cargo is His Majesty's property."

"Are the lions big?" Don Quixote asked.

"They're the biggest that have ever crossed from Africa to Spain," the lion keeper said. "I should know.

I have transported many other lions before, but none like these. The one in the front cage is the male, the other the female. Right now they are very hungry; they haven't had a thing to eat all day. . . . So, Your Lordship, I suggest you move away and let us go. These animals need to be fed soon."

Don Quixote smiled with pure joy. "Lions, a couple of puny lions should scare me, eh?" he said. "Good man, since you are the lion keeper, open the cages and let those beasts out. I will show them who Don Quixote de la Mancha is, in spite of the wizards who have sent them to me."

The man in the green coat mumbled: "No doubt about it, either the man is crazy or the cottage cheese softened his brain!"

Sancho, who heard his remark, said, "No, he's not crazy, just bold."

Everybody wanted to convince Don Quixote that it was foolhardy to face the lions. Actually, it was suicide, they said. But all talk failed, and those present scattered as fast and as far away as they could before the cage was opened. Sancho cried deep, heartfelt tears. "Oh, my master, my friend, is going to become a lion's dinner," he said between sobs.

Under threat, then, the lion keeper opened one cage. Don Quixote thought for a minute. Should he face the lion on horseback or on foot? On foot, he decided; "Rocinante might get scared by the sight of the lion."

The lion turned around in his cage, then stretched. He opened his mouth and yawned, then showed a

huge tongue and cleaned his face with it. Next he stuck his face out of the cage and looked around, his eyes like burning coals. Don Quixote stared at him. He wished with all his heart that the beast would jump on him so he could strangle it with his bare hands.

The lion, on the other hand, wasn't interested. He turned around, showed his back to the knight, and sat down again in his cage.

Don Quixote was furious. He wanted the lion keeper to make the lion mad. The lion keeper said he would not: "No, Your Lordship; the lion had the cage open and didn't feel like coming out. You have proved beyond all doubt that you are a brave and courageous man. The lion didn't want to fight; the shame is on him."

Don Quixote was satisfied with this reasoning, and called all the others. They were dumfounded at seeing him in one piece, without even a scratch! The lion keeper filled them in on the details of what they had missed, actions and words. "As soon as I arrive at the Court, I will personally tell His Majesty of Don Quixote's courage," he said.

Sancho, on Don Quixote's orders, gave the driver and the lion keeper a little money to make up for the delay. The men went happily on their way, relieved that nothing had happened when they had expected the worst.

From now on, Don Quixote announced, "I shall proudly bear the title 'Knight of the Lions' next to my own name."

CHAPTER 11

The Puppet Show

One day, Don Quixote and Sancho stopped at an inn. Later on, a man with a green eye patch came to the same place. He wanted a room, and the innkeeper, on recognizing him, said, "Of course. I'd give you a room if I had to take it away from the most powerful duke in Spain."

The man went back outside for his belongings. Don Quixote wanted to know who that stranger, so well received, was.

"He's a very famous puppeteer, that Master Peter," said the innkeeper. "He goes from town to town with a puppet show and a most unusual monkey, who can answer questions. The animal knows about the present and the past! You ask him a question, he jumps on his master's shoulder and whispers the answer. Master Peter then tells you what the animal said."

The man came back at that moment. The monkey got on his shoulder and started whispering, without being asked any questions. Master Peter got on his knees in front of Don Quixote. Hugging the knight's knees, he said, "I embrace the knees of the most famous of all knights, Don Quixote de la Mancha, fighter of evil and savior of the unfortunate."

How surprised Don Quixote was!

The man went on, "You, Sancho Panza, are the best squire of the best knight in the world!"

Sancho's eyes were as big as saucers.

"Now, in honor of you both and the other people at this inn," said Master Peter, "we're going to have a puppet show."

The stage was set. Master Peter went behind the scenes to handle the puppets. A young boy stood by the side to explain the action and show with a pointer the different figures that were coming on stage.

There was a blast of drums and trumpets.

"This is the true story of Doña Melisendra, wife of Don Gaiferos, on the occasion of her rescue from the prison in which the Moors had her in Spain," the boy said. "Emperor Charlemagne, Melisendra's father, is coming to scold his son-in-law Don Gaiferos for wasting his time playing chess. Now Don Gaiferos runs to her rescue! He comes to the tower where she's held prisoner. Now Don Gaiferos arrives; Doña Melisendra climbs down the balcony and jumps on her husband's horse."

The boy kept pointing at the puppets moving around the stage. He went on: "Oh, what bad luck! Her skirt gets caught in the iron bars of the balcony. She's hanging, not able to reach the floor! Don Gaiferos grabs her and puts her on his horse; he asks her to hold tight so she doesn't fall. Look at that horse fleeing! But King Marsilio has been warned and starts pursuing the couple. I'm afraid he's going to catch up with them and bring them back tied to his horse's tail, and that's terrible!!!"

Don Quixote stood up and shouted: "I won't let that happen in my presence to the brave knight Don Gaiferos. Stop, you villains! Don't pursue him if you don't want to face me in combat!"

Then with his sword, he tore all the puppets in the show. Heads, legs, arms, flew in all directions.

"They're not *real* Moors, they're just puppets!" Master Peter cried. "You're ruining my show! You're ruining me!"

The confusion was monumental. The monkey ran away. Sancho was scared—he'd never seen his master *so* angry before.

All finished with his task, Don Quioxote calmed down and said, "I'd like to see before me all those who claim that knights do no good. I have just saved Don Gaiferos and Doña Melisendra from the wicked Moors. Long live knighthood!"

Master Peter was crying real tears. Sancho, saddened by those tears, told him that his master would pay for all the damage.

And Don Quixote agreed to pay, but he also said that he was more convinced than ever that wizards were playing tricks on him. It was not the first time that he believed what the eyes of his imagination saw instead of what was real.

Sancho and Master Peter made an estimate of the damage, and Don Quixote paid every last bit of it. All was well and forgotten. They had dinner together.

But who was that Master Peter? Remember the cocky Ginés de Pasamonte, one of the convicts freed by Don Quixote? This was the same man, now disguised with the eye patch. At this time, he made a living with his traveling puppet show and the monkey fortuneteller.

It was rumored that, before he entered a town, he would ask a few people in the vicinity what was news in the area. That way, the monkey would "know" what to tell. And that's why he could tell only about the past and the present, not the future. But in the case of Don Quixote and Sancho, no one had to tell anything to anyone. Ginés de Pasamonte remembered them very well.

CHAPTER 12

At the Duke's Palace

After leaving the inn, Don Quixote and Sancho traveled around the countryside for a while. One day, near a wood, they saw a large hunting party. A beautiful lady, mounted on a magnificent white horse, was in the center of it.

"Sancho, go to that beautiful lady," Don Quixote said. "Tell her that I, the Knight of the Lions, kiss her hands and am willing to serve her with the strength of my arms if Her Highness permits."

Sancho went and introduced himself. The beautiful hunter didn't let him remain on his knees, for he was the squire of a very famous knight, she said.

"Tell your master that he is welcome. He may come and serve me and my husband, the Duke, in a palace we have near here."

"So beautiful," Sancho thought, "and so sweet." He brought the message to Don Quixote, who immediately ran to meet her.

She, meanwhile, had called the Duke aside. They decided to amuse themselves by treating Don Quixote in the manner the novels of knighthood said knights should be treated.

The Duke, the Duchess, and Don Quixote rode toward the palace. Sancho and the rest of the party followed. The Duke himself went ahead of the others to prepare the palace for the guests' arrival!

When Don Quixote got off his horse, two beautiful ladies put a scarlet robe on his shoulders. Then the corridors filled with servants chanting, "Welcome to the flower and cream of knighthood!" And they sprayed perfume over him, the Duke, and the Duchess. In a big hall full of silk and brocade, six ladies helped him take off his armor. After that, twelve pages escorted him to a richly decorated table with four settings. Everybody had a hard time keeping from laughing at the knight and the squire.

There was a grave-looking clergyman with the Duke and Duchess in the dining room. Don Quixote was asked to sit at the head of the table. The clergyman sat opposite him, the Duke on one side, the Duchess on another.

The Duchess wanted to know about Dulcinea. "Have you sent her any giants lately to pay respects, dear Don Quixote?" she asked.

"Yes, Your Highness," he confessed, "but my luck is such that one of my enemies has transformed her into an ordinary farm girl."

The serious-minded priest, hearing all that talk about giants and enchantments, imagined that this must be the hero of the book the Duke liked to read often. So he said to Don Quixote, "Who has told you that you are a knight, you fool? Who has charged you with the job of fighting evil creatures? Go back to

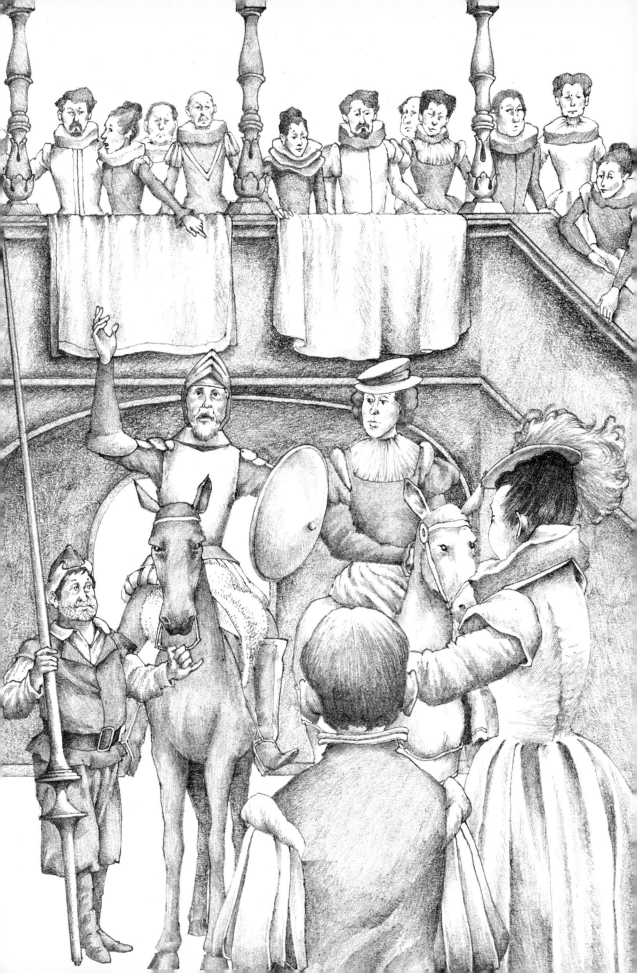

your home, take care of your children and spouse, and of your affairs. Stop roaming around, being everybody's laughingstock!"

Don Quixote stood up, shaking from head to toe. "Be thankful that I respect your priestly state," he said. "But tell me, Your Grace, why do you order me to take care of wife and children without knowing whether I have any? Going through the world righting wrongs and punishing evil is no easy task, but it is satisfying work. And if I am called a fool for that, say something in my defense, Honorable Duke and Duchess."

The priest addressed the squire next. "Are you, by chance, that Sancho Panza to whom his master promised an island to govern?"

"Yes, Your Holiness," Sancho answered. "And I deserve it as much as anyone."

Host and hostess were having the time of their lives. They would not let the priest spoil their fun. The Duke said to Sancho, "Sancho, my friend, I, in the name of the great Don Quixote, appoint you governor of one of my islands."

"Kneel, Sancho," commanded Don Quixote, "and kiss His Highness' feet."

Sancho did as told. The priest could not take it any longer. "You are *all* crazy," he said. "I shall not set foot in this palace as long as those foolish guests remain here."

CHAPTER 13

The Adventure of the Wooden Horse

Everyone at the palace was having a grand time playing tricks on the knight and the squire. The Duke and Duchess played many themselves, and they also encouraged their servants to come up with ideas of their own.

One good afternoon, while Duke, Duchess, and guests were in the garden, twelve young ladies came in two lines. Following them was an older lady. All thirteen had their faces covered by thick black veils.

The older lady said they were looking for Don Quixote de la Mancha and Sancho Panza. Her voice was a little deep, but no one paid much attention to that. She said she had heard of the knight's courage and deeds. Both Sancho and Don Quixote stood up and identified themselves.

She said she was Countess Trifaldi, governess of Princess Antonomasia, from the kingdom of Candaya. The very young princess fell in love with Don Clavijo, and on her own agreed to be his wife. But Don Clavijo was only a knight, and Princess Antonomasia was

the heir to the throne. Then, one day, giant Malambruno, a wizard, came riding a wooden horse and
turned Antonomasia into a bronze monkey and Clavijo
into a crocodile of an unknown metal. The giant left a
note saying: "They shall not return to their natural
shapes until the brave knight from La Mancha himself
fights me."

Countess Trifaldi explained that she and the ladies
who served in the palace had been punished too: they
all grew beards overnight. They lifted their veils and
showed.

Don Quixote was moved. He could not see that
these were not women but men dressed in women's
clothing. He promised to save them all. Countess Trifaldi said that Malambruno would send a flying wooden
horse to take the knight to fight with him. It was a
horse made for two, a horse for knight and squire. The
horse was named Clavileño. His reins were wooden
pegs. "He's very swift, Your Grace," she said.

Sancho was unhappy about this trip. He wanted to
stay with the Duchess when his master went to fight,
but Don Quixote said he must go or the spell wouldn't
be broken.

Clavileño came on the shoulders of four big, mon-
strous-looking men. One of the monsters said both
riders should be blindfolded and should remain blindfolded until the horse neighed.

Don Quixote mounted willingly, Sancho less willingly. The master squeezed the wooden peg, and the
veiled "women" started shouting their good wishes.

"God be with you."

"Look at that—fast as an arrow."

"Sancho, hold tight, don't fall."

"Master," Sancho asked, "how can we be flying so high if we can still hear their voices?"

"This is no ordinary adventure," Don Quixote answered. "Don't pay attention to that. Don't be afraid, Sancho."

"Master, I feel so much air; it feels like bellows."

Sancho was right; the pranksters were using bellows to make the riders believe they were flying. But Don Quixote said they were arriving at the second region of space, where hail and snow come from. "After this, in the third region, there's fire," he predicted.

In spite of the fun they were having, the people thought it was time to end the episode. They set fire to Clavileño's tail. The horse was full of firecrackers; it flew into hundreds of pieces. Don Quixote and Sancho were thrown to the ground, half scorched.

Knight and squire got up in pitiful shape. They were astonished to see themselves in the same garden they had left. So many people were lying on the ground, too! They were even more astonished when they saw this sign hanging from a lance:

THE RENOWNED DON QUIXOTE DE LA MANCHA ENDED THE ADVENTURE OF COUNTESS TRIFALDI ON THE FIRST TRY. MALAMBRUNO IS SATISFIED. THE BEARDS OF THE YOUNG WOMEN ARE GONE. DON CLAVIJO AND DOÑA ANTONOMASIA ARE RETURNED TO THEIR PREVIOUS SHAPES.

The Duke and Duchess "woke up," as "surprised" as the others. The Duke read the sign, too, and with open arms went to embrace Don Quixote, "the best knight of all times."

Sancho was asked about the trip. "Oh, I saw many stars . . . some looked like little bears," he said.

Duke and Duchess would have something to laugh about for a long time, and Sancho, something to remember and talk about all his life.

CHAPTER 14

Don Quixote
Advises Sancho

It was time for Sancho to go to the island, and the Duke asked him to get ready.

"I don't have to get any special clothing," Sancho said. "In any fashion, I'm the same old Sancho Panza."

"True," said the Duke. "Still, one should dress according to what one does—a soldier doesn't dress like a priest, and a lawyer doesn't dress like a soldier."

The decision was that part of Sancho's wardrobe would be like that of a lawyer or judge, and part like a military uniform. But Sancho said there and then that he would not part with his own poor clothes; he would take them with him.

Don Quixote asked for permission to be alone with Sancho. He wanted to talk to the new governor in private. Most of all, he wanted to give him advice for his new life. These are some of the words of advice he gave:

"Sancho, my son, I thank heaven for your happiness, which you have found even before I found my reward. If you look at it carefully, it is just luck. I'm telling you this because I don't want you to think it's your worth alone."

Sancho was paying strict attention. Don Quixote continued, "First of all, my son, you should fear God. Fear of God is wisdom, and with wisdom you cannot make mistakes.

"Second, you should put your eyes upon yourself,

that is, you should know yourself, which is the most difficult knowledge of all. If you know yourself, you don't put on airs; if you do put them on, it will only come out that you were a swineherd before. Be proud of what you are. You should never be ashamed of your family of farmers and laborers. No one will make fun of you if you are proud of yourself and your relatives.

"Look, Sancho, you should always do good, and not envy anyone who has more than you. Material things are acquired, and virtue is more valuable than material things.

"If a relative of yours comes to the island while you're governor, treat him or her very well. If you bring your wife with you, teach her, because she's not educated. Help her to be polite. Manners are important for people in public life.

"A poor person's tears should make you feel pity, but if a rich person complaining about the poor one is right, you should do justice.

"Always try to discover the truth through the promises and gifts of a rich person as well as through the sobs of a poor one.

"When you must apply the law, do not impose all the weight of it on the convict. It is better to be compassionate than too stern.

"If you must pass sentence on a matter in which an enemy of yours is involved, forget you are not friends. Look only at the truth of the matter.

"Above all, Sancho, be devout and merciful. God likes mercy.

"If you follow these rules, you shall live a long life, and become famous throughout the world. That's all I'm telling you about spiritual matters. Now let me give you advice about manners.

"The first thing you must remember is to be clean and clip your fingernails. Don't be sloppy. People will think you're disorganized if they see you unkempt.

"Don't eat garlic and onion, especially when you have to meet people. The smell will tell you're not well bred.

"Don't overeat. Health is tied to the stomach!

"Don't drink too much, either. It is not very wise.

"Don't take too big a bite and don't belch in front of others.

"Don't oversleep. Get up early and enjoy the day. Remember that hard work breeds good luck, and laziness its opposite.

"And one more thing. Don't ever discuss family backgrounds, or compare one with another. No one is better than anyone else. You only stand to make enemies when you make comparisons.

"This is all for now, Sancho. Later on, when there's need, I'll give you more advice."

Sancho spoke at long last.

"Master, all the things you said are good, I guess, but what good will they do me? I won't remember half of them. Give them to me written down. You know I don't know how to read, but I can give them to someone like the priest to read to me."

"Heaven help us! You can't read!" Don Quixote exclaimed. "This is wrong. A governor should know how to read and write! I am serious, Sancho. I want you to learn."

"Well, master, I know how to sign my name," Sancho said. "Later, later."

"May the Almighty guide you in your governorship, Sancho," his master said. "Let's leave it here. If you are a bad governor, it will be your fault, but the shame will be mine."

Sancho worried about those final words. "Master, if Your Grace thinks I'm not qualified, I'm resigning right here and now. If the devil is going to take me for being governor, I prefer to go to heaven being my own self: Sancho Panza."

"Enough, Sancho," Don Quixote said. "You make me very proud. You are capable of being a good governor, not of one but of many islands."

CHAPTER 15

Sancho, Governor for Life

$\mathbf{S}$ancho left for the "island," a gentleman on a fine horse. The Duke's butler and a large group escorted him. Rucio, the donkey, walked behind, adorned with ribbons and bows. His owner turned back occasionally to look at him fondly.

They soon arrived in a village of about one thousand people. This was, Sancho was told, "Barataria Island." The truth is, it was not an island at all. It was just one of those small towns and villages that used to be under a nobleman's protection. The nobleman in this case was the Duke. Like many other towns and villages in the old days, this one was surrounded by walls as protection against enemies.

The villagers had been told of Sancho's arrival. Everybody was there to greet him, and the church bells rang in celebration. There was a big thanksgiving service in the church, and at the end of it, Sancho was given the keys to the town in a most ridiculous ceremony.

"We hereby declare you, Honorable Sancho Panza,

Governor for Life of Barataria Island," said a man who called himself an alderman.

"Long live our Governor for Life," the people cried.

From the church he was taken to the courthouse. The next part of the ceremony called for the new governor to answer a few difficult questions. "That's the way for people to know what kind of governor they have," the Duke's butler said. "If he's smart, the people are happy; if he's stupid, they're sad."

Several cases were brought before His Honor. There were many quarrels among people who didn't get along with one another. And there was an interesting case, a dispute between a tailor and a farmer.

"Your Honor," the tailor said, "this man brought me a piece of cloth for me to make a cape for him. Then he said he wanted two capes out of the same piece of fabric. Then he said, 'Make me three,' then, 'Make me four,' then, 'Make me five.' I made his five capes. Now he comes to get them and he doesn't want to pay me."

"Is the tailor telling the truth?" Sancho asked the farmer.

"Well, your Honor, I did ask him to make a cape, and in the end, I asked for five," said the farmer. "But, Your Honor, ask him to show you what he made. The capes are so little they are useless. They are only good for children to play with."

The tailor showed the five capes, five tiny capes. Everyone wondered which man would win the case. Sancho thought for a minute and said, "The whole episode seems ridiculous. One man didn't give all the information needed; he didn't give measurements, he didn't give sizes. The other one didn't even bother to ask for the information. My decision is: the farmer loses his cloth and the tailor loses his work. The case is closed."

The people were very surprised at their governor. They had not expected a man who would reason so well. But, then, Sancho had a lot of common sense.

From the courthouse, Sancho and the official party went to the palace that was to become his residence.

CHAPTER 16

Danger at the Island

The governor's palace was large and rich. Sancho arrived to the sound of trumpets. He was greeted by four pages, who escorted him to the dining room. There was a large table—overflowing with delicious dishes—and only one chair. A page put a bib on him, another placed a bowl of fresh fruit before him. Sancho had taken only one bite when a man standing beside him touched the plate with a stick and, presto, the bowl was removed.

The butler brought another plate. Sancho didn't even get a taste before the man with the stick had it taken away. The governor was annoyed. What kind of game was this? The man of the stick said, "Sir, I am the official physician of the governor of this island. I am present at all his meals. I make sure he is healthy and fit. I do not allow him to eat what I do not consider good for him."

"In that case," Sancho said, "those partridges will be fine for me."

"Don't even mention them," the doctor said. "Our great Hippocrates, the father of medicine, says that a bellyful is bad, and if it is a bellyful of partridges, it is worse."

"Well, Mr. Doctor, find something good for me to eat. I'm starving. . . . How about some of that beef stew?" he asked.

"Strictly forbidden!" answered the doctor. "There is nothing worse than beef stew."

Now Sancho was really angry. Looking at the doctor—sizing him up—from head to toe, he roared: "YOU QUACK, OUT OF MY SIGHT! Quick, or I'll have all doctors in this island beaten to death on your account! Move, I said, or I'll break this chair on your head! I want food—or I give up the governorship. A job that doesn't feed you is not worth two peas!"

The doctor was scared; he was leaving. But in came the butler, running, all excited, with a letter from the Duke. The envelope read: "To the Honorable Don Sancho Panza, Governor of Barataria Island, in his own hands or in the hands of his secretary."

Inside, the message was:

I have learned, Honorable Don Sancho Panza, that some enemies of mine in that island are planning an attack one of these evenings. My advice is: be on the alert to avoid surprises. I have also learned that four persons—in disguise—have entered the island with the intention of killing you. Take precautions; pay attention to those who come to talk to you. Also, don't eat anything given to you. I will be prepared to come to your aid if necessary.

This message is so urgent that it has been written at 4 A.M.

Your friend,

(signed) The Duke

Some news! Sancho turned to the butler and said, "What we must do now is jail the doctor. If anyone is trying to kill me, it's got to be him."

"I'm also of the opinion," the butler said, "that Your Honor should not eat the things on the table. Who knows? They may be poisoned."

"Well, then," Sancho said, "bring me bread and grapes. I cannot go without food. I must be prepared for any battle."

CHAPTER 17

Sancho's Wisest Decision

On the night of Sancho's seventh day as governor, just when he began to fall asleep, there was a great commotion outside: bells ringing, people shouting, as if the island were going under. More noise; trumpets and drums.

Sancho peeked out his bedroom door. About twenty people carrying torches were coming toward his room, shouting, "To arms! To arms, Your Honor! This island is under enemy attack! We need your strength, your ingenuity, your courage to guide us!"

At the door, one said to him, "Take up arms, your Honor, or we'll lose the entire island!"

"Why should I take up arms?" Sancho replied. "I don't know a thing about combat. That's my master Don Quixote's business, not mine."

"Take up arms, Your Grace," said another. "Be our guide and leader."

"All right, all right, I'll take up arms," Sancho reluctantly agreed.

They brought two shields and put the governor between them, like a sandwich, then tied some string around it all. It was impossible for him to move, walk,

or even bend his knees! They gave him a lance; he used it to help himself stand up.

"Lead us, Your Honor. Lead us, Your Honor," they chanted.

"How do you think I can lead you?" Sancho protested. "Like this, the best I can do is stand in front of a door or window to block it."

"Come on, Sir Governor! Fear doesn't let you move," someone taunted.

Sancho tried to move but fell down. Like a turtle or a snail in his shell! And then those heartless people blew out the torches and ran around, shouting, walking all over him, stabbing the shields as if they were enemies on the attack. It was a frightening and dangerous moment for this simple peasant turned governor.

Poor Sancho prayed, "God Almighty, if you could only finish this fight. I don't care if the island is lost. All I want is to be free from this agony."

And then he heard the cries: "Victory, victory! Get up, Sir Governor. Come enjoy our victory. Let's go divide the booty."

"We owe it all to you, our courageous governor," someone whispered in his ear.

"Help me," Sancho pleaded. "I don't want any part of any booty. All I want is a friend, if I have any, to bring me something to drink and wipe my face."

A helping hand wiped his face, gave him a drink, and freed him from the prison of the shields. Then he fainted! The pranksters were beginning to feel sorry for what they had done—had they played too dirty a trick?—when Sancho came to. He asked what time it was. It was almost daybreak.

Silently he got up, dressed, and went to the stables in a hurry, followed by a few curiosity seekers. He went straight to his donkey, kissed its face, and said, "My friend and companion, when my only worry was to take care of you, I was a happy man. But I left you. I became too ambitious and uppity, and I became miserable, and I have suffered for it."

As he talked, he was harnessing the donkey. Still very sore from what had happened to him, he mounted. Then he tearfully addressed the butler, the doctor, and all the others: "Make way, gentlemen; let me go back to my freedom. I was not born to be governor or to defend islands from enemies. I know more about farming than about laws and defense. I also prefer to eat soup than to be subjected to the grip of a doctor who wants to kill me by starving me to death. Please let me go; I have a few broken ribs—the enemy stepped on me last night."

"Sir Governor, don't worry," said the doctor. "I'll prepare a good medicine for you. And about the food, I'll let you eat everything you want and as much as you want."

"It's too late for that, my friend," Sancho replied. "Pranks like those are played only once. I am a Panza. In my family, when one says no, it's no. Let me go; it's getting late."

The butler said, "We would let you go, even if we're losing you, but every governor must account for his administration."

"Nobody can ask me for any account," Sancho snapped, "except the Duke himself or a person *he* names. I'm on my way to see the Duke. Besides, look at me. Look at my clothes. I have only what belongs to me. I have behaved like an angel."

"The great Sancho is right," the doctor said. "I think we should let him go. The Duke will be glad to see him."

They let him go. They even offered him escort and anything he wanted for his trip. His only request was barley for the donkey and half a loaf of bread and a little cheese for himself.

Sancho was a man without schooling. Yet he was a wise man. He found out he could not handle the job, and he had the courage to resign.

The villagers, with the Duke's knowledge and encouragement, had played a lot of tricks on their governor, and they had had fun. But, at the end, they truly admired Sancho Panza as a human being.

CHAPTER 18

Knight and Squire Reunited

Darkness came while Sancho was still a little way from the palace of the Duke and Duchess. He took a path on the side of the main road, intending to spend the night outdoors and start again in the morning. But the donkey came up to a canyonlike cave . . . and fell in. Frightened at first and then relieved because neither was hurt, Sancho started thinking. "How are we ever going to get out of here?" he asked himself out loud.

Meanwhile, Don Quixote was restless at the palace. He missed his squire, his friend. His life was too soft. That morning, he went for a ride in the countryside. And he heard a voice coming from deep down in the earth. The voice seemed familiar. Could it be . . . ?

"Who's down there? Who's complaining?" he asked.

"Who could it be but beat-up Sancho Panza!" said the voice. "The unfortunate governor of Barataria Island, formerly the squire of the famous knight Don Quixote de la Mancha."

This cannot be, Don Quixote thought. Perhaps San-

cho was dead and this was his soul speaking. So he said, "If you are a spirit, tell me what you want me to do for you. My profession is to help the needy in this world. I suppose I can also do something for the needy in the other world."

"Then," said the voice from below, "you are my master, Don Quixote de la Mancha! I recognize your voice!"

"I am Don Quixote, certainly. Tell me who you are. You have me confused. If you are the soul of my dead squire, Sancho Panza, I can have a few masses said for your eternal peace."

"Wouldn't you know it! Master, Knight Don Quixote de la Mancha, I swear I am your squire, Sancho Panza, alive as can be. I left the governship—I'll tell you why later—and I fell in this cave, with my donkey. He'll tell you too."

The donkey neighed!

"Oh, yes, I recognize your donkey's neigh! Sancho wait; I'll go back to the palace; I'll be back soon with help!"

After the rescue, a happy pair returned to the palace. The Duke and Duchess were waiting for them. But first things first: Sancho went to the stables to take care of his donkey.

Then he returned to the palace, where he said a speech:

"I, Your Highnesses, went to govern Barataria Island because you are very generous, not because I deserve it. I went there dressed poorly; dressed poorly I am now. You may want to know if I was a good governor. There are witnesses who can tell you whatever they want. I settled disputes, I cleared doubts; that is, I did my job. While I was governor, I almost died of hunger because the doctor wouldn't let me eat. One night, the enemy came. The citizens are now saying that my bravery brought victory, but they are not truthful. In short, I found out that I cannot carry on my shoulders the obligations and duties of a governor. Yesterday morning, I left the island. It remained exactly as I found it: same streets, houses, roofs, everything there was when I got there."

That was all. Don Quixote was relieved: his beloved squire spoke well, and he was safe.

"I am sorry you left the governorship so soon," the Duke said. "I can give you another job of less responsibility and more suited to you, if you wish." But Sancho said no, he had had enough.

The Duke and Duchess hugged him and ordered that he be treated very nicely and comfortably.

CHAPTER 19

The Knight of the White Moon

Life at the palace was not satisfying. Don Quixote kept thinking of the needy people in the world who could use his help. One day, he secured permission to leave, and knight and squire took to the road again.

"Freedom, Sancho, is one of the greatest gifts heaven can give a person. Nothing can compare with it, not the riches deep in the earth, nor the riches deep in the sea. One's freedom, and one's honor, are as important as life itself. Captivity, on the contrary, is the worst evil that can fall on a person. I am telling you this, Sancho, because you saw and experienced the great life we had at the palace. But I can now tell you that, in the middle of those grand banquets, I felt hungry, because I was not free. Those were not *my* delicacies. Happy is the person who has a piece of bread and only has to thank heaven for it."

"Well, master," the practical Sancho said, "we should not be ungrateful to the Duke. His butler gave me this little bag with two hundred gold coins in it. We're not going to find palaces all over; we may need to stay at a few inns."

Don Quixote decided to head for Barcelona, a beautiful city by the sea.

One morning, Don Quixote, dressed in full armor, was riding along the beach. Suddenly a knight came toward him, also dressed in full armor, a shining moon painted on his shield. When he was within hearing distance he intoned:

"Famous Don Quixote de la Mancha, knight who has not yet been recognized in all his worth! I am the Knight of the White Moon. No doubt you have heard of my deeds. I am here to fight with you, to test the strength of your arms, to make you confess that my lady—anyone I choose for my lady—is infinitely more beautiful than your Dulcinea. If you confess this truth immediately, you will not die at my hand; you will spare me the trouble of killing you. If we fight and I win, I only want you to abandon your armor and stop looking for adventure. I want you to go back to your home town and live there in peace for an entire year, without touching a sword, because you need to look after your estate and you need to rest. If you win, my head will be at your disposal, and my armor and horse will be yours, and my fame will be added to yours. Tell me what is your wish; I want to finish this business today."

"How arrogant, that Knight of the White Moon," Don Quixote thought, "and what a ridiculous cause for a challenge! No beauty comes near Dulcinea's." He said calmly and gravely, "Knight of the White Moon, I have not heard of you before, and I will make you vow that you have never seen Dulcinea del Toboso.

You would not have made your foolish remarks if you had seen her. I accept your challenge, with one exception: I do not want your fame added to mine, because I don't know about your deeds. Let's go on with it, then. Take the side of the field you prefer."

Don Quixote prayed to God and thought of Dulcinea. He was ready.

They headed toward each other. The Knight of the White Moon had a faster horse; Don Quixote fell off Rocinante without even being touched by his opponent's lance. Planting his lance on Don Quixote's helmet, the victor said, "You are beaten, Sir Knight Don Quixote de la Mancha, and you'll die if you do not confess what we agreed upon."

Don Quixote would rather die. With a deep voice, as if coming from the other world, he said, "Dulcinea del Toboso is the most beautiful woman in the world, and I am the most unfortunate knight on earth. Her name and her honor are not to suffer because I am weak. Go on, Sir Knight of the White Moon, drive the lance through; take my life, since you have taken my honor."

"I shall not!" said the Knight of the White Moon. "Long live the beauty of Doña Dulcinea del Toboso, lady of the brave knight Don Quixote de la Mancha! I am content with the second part of the pledge: Don Quixote shall return to his home town for a year, or as long as I say, as agreed before the fight."

"Anything not against my lady Dulcinea del Toboso I will do as a true gentleman," he replied humbly, sadly.

Don Quixote was numb; Sancho, sad and confused. Was this a bad dream, a nightmare? What was going to happen? One whole year without taking up arms! What about Rocinante? And what about his master? Was he badly hurt? "O God, please let this be only a nightmare," he prayed.

Don Quixote was bedridden for a few days. He was not wounded, but he was feverish. And in his better moments, one thought kept coming to his mind: Who was the Knight of the White Moon? He had never heard of him. He had no idea that it was none other than his friend Samson Carrasco! The young man, the priest, and the barber had never stopped thinking of ways to make their friend go back to a normal life at home. This time, they had succeeded.

When Don Quixote recovered, it was time to go home. The knight wore regular clothes; his armor was put over Sancho's donkey. His faithful squire walked all the way home to La Mancha.

CHAPTER 20

Don Quixote's Last Illness

It may have been heartbreak, or just fate, but Don Quixote developed a very high fever. He was in bed for six days. His friends the priest, the barber, and Samson came to see him many times daily. Sancho, his good friend and faithful squire, didn't go far for long. They were all trying to cheer him up, but it couldn't be done.

One day, they had to call the doctor. He took Don Quixote's pulse. He told the patient to take care of his spiritual needs, because his life was in danger. Don Quixote took the news calmly, but not so his niece, his housekeeper, and Sancho. On hearing the bad news, they sobbed for a long time.

Don Quixote asked to be left alone. He slept six straight hours. When he woke up, he asked his niece to call his three best friends. He wanted to make confession, he said, and to dictate his last will and testament. But there was no need to call the friends; they walked in.

Don Quixote said to them: "Rejoice, my friends, I

am no longer Don Quixote de la Mancha but Alonso Quixano. I now hate tales of knighthood and recognize that reading them put me in danger. My time has come. I want to make confession. Also, bring me a scribe to write my last will and testament."

The friends looked at one another. They had not expected this shocking news. All but the priest left the room, and the confession took place. Then Samson brought the scribe. Sancho, niece, and housekeeper could not stop sobbing.

Don Quixote began, "First, it is my will that, out of my estate, my niece pay the salary owed my housekeeper for the length of her service to me, plus a little extra for a new dress. Second, it is also my will that Sancho keep for himself a little money he's holding for me, and that no one ask him to account for it. In my madness, I made him my squire, and was instrumental in getting him an island to govern. Now that I am sane, I would give him an entire kingdom if I could."

Turning to Sancho, he said, "Forgive me, my friend, because I, being crazy, made you seem crazy too."

"Master, master, don't die." Sancho said between sobs. "Don't let yourself die. You taught me to fight for what one believes in! Fight for your life!"

"Sancho is right, dear friend. Listen to him," Samson said.

Don Quixote paid no attention. "I was crazy before, and now I am sane," he said. "I pray that you all forgive me. Please, scribe, let's continue with the will.

"It is my last will that my niece, Antonia Quixano, be the one and only heir of my estate. Should my niece, Antonia Quixano, want to marry, she is to marry a man who is not acquainted with tales of knighthood. If her love knows those books about knights, and she insists on marrying him, my entire estate shall be given to charity. I hereby name the priest and Samson Carrasco executors of my will."

Don Quixote fainted. His loved ones were in turmoil. Yet he lived for three more days, three more days in which he constantly said how much he hated those books that had made him crazy; he also took the last sacraments.

The end was peaceful. Samson Carrasco wrote an epitaph for the grave. It was a poem that said, in part, that Don Quixote was a good man, brave to the last moment, and that he will be remembered forever in the entire world for having lived crazy and died sane.